HOOSIER NOIR

VOL. 5

Editor: N.B. Turner

Copyright © 2022 Hoosier Noir

All rights reserved.

ISBN: 9798359300940

Copyright © 2022 Hoosier Noir All rights reserved.

The characters and events portrayed in this book are fictitious. Any similarity to real persons, living or dead, is coincidental and not intended by the author.

No part of this book may be reproduced, or stored in a retrieval system, or transmitted in any form or by any means, electronic, mechanical, photocopying, recording, or otherwise, without express written permission of the publisher.

CONTENTS

FOREWORD

To our readers,

We are grateful that you've purchased this issue of Hoosier Noir. Whether this is your first time reading, or you've been a long-time subscriber, we plan to show you something unique. Within these pages, there is crime, horror, intrigue, and people just trying to make their way in a world that often doesn't give a damn for their feelings of right and wrong. They offer a portrait of a state which gets a bad rap for being simple, when really, it's anything but.

To kick off, Shari Held's *The Good Girl* gives a story of blackmail, secrets, and intrigue befitting the back alleys of Washington, D.C., but taking place in Indianapolis. Things are darker than they appear on the surface here, and sometimes justice needs some underhanded help.

Next, Veronica Leigh takes you back to Indiana in the 1930s, a period of history many may try to forget. *Strange Fruit* can appear on the trees in this state, once known for having one of the largest Klan memberships in the country. Inspired by historical events, including one that inspired the song of the same by Billie Holiday, the work shows one woman trying to comprehend how "good people" could tolerate a hatred that would kill people for nothing more than the color of their skin. It shows that some sins are so heinous that they spread like a virus and corrupt even those who didn't commit them.

For a short interlude, Brian Beatty gives three stories from a sequence of vignettes from one man's life: *Chicago That One Time, Winner Winner,* and *Turkey Nights.* For Hurley, it's about making it through the day: sometimes you need to fight as a gas station, others you win the lottery, but it's all just part of making it through the next sunrise.

The penultimate story for this issue takes place in Gary, a town whose better days gave the world steel and The Jackson 5 and now has a reputation for abandoned buildings and high crime. But Danny Sophabismay's *DWB* shows that sometimes the criminals are kinder than the cops, and that first impressions only show a portion of the truth.

Last, but not least, Matthew X. Gomez gives a horror story called *Rust Belt Revenant.* Revenge is a tricky business: sometimes you pay a higher price than you expected. Getting out is never as simple as you hope, and ghosts can haunt you long after.

Our home of Indiana, despite its lack of heights, contains a depth of stories. Mining those depths is like mining for diamonds, and we've found some gems to show you, dear reader. We hope you enjoy them.

Shari Held

THE GOOD GIRL

Lena Langtree rolled off the man next to her at the JW Marriott, propped herself up on one elbow, and studied him. Jeffrey Smythe's eyes were closed, and he huffed and puffed like he'd just run a marathon. His eyes fluttered open as she traced the tiger line of his chest hair with a scarlet fingernail. She rewarded him with a languid, self-satisfied smile. It was genuine, but it didn't result from their bedroom acrobatics.

Smythe sighed, closed his eyes, and placed his hand, the one with the wedding ring, on her bare thigh. "You're something else, Sissie." He scrambled to an upright position, slid off the side of the bed, and collected his clothes. "I know better than to offer you money, but I booked the spa for you. The works. Just give them the room number and they'll put it on my tab."

"Oh, thank you," Lena cooed, looking up at him adoringly as she tamped down the urge to roll her eyes. "You're the best."

He finished dressing, then drew her close. "God, you're beautiful, Sissie. I'll never know how a guy like me landed time with a girl like you." He nuzzled her breasts, then gave her a sloppy kiss before leaving.

The minute she heard the door click Lena jumped into action. "A girl like you," she repeated. "If only you knew." She slipped on her underwear, jeans, and sweater and pulled her long auburn hair into a ponytail. She had what she needed from Smythe. No repeats of their afternoon delight sessions would be necessary.

Lena retrieved the camera she'd hooked up on the armoire. She'd drop it by Gregory's apartment later. By the time her tech guy did his magic, she'd have four hours of erotic entertainment for Mrs. Smythe, starring her husband and "Sissie."

Lena laughed. Family was everything to Smythe and his uptight, holier-than-thou wife. That video would poison their marital bliss. Smythe would soon feel what it was like to have his family ripped apart.

Lena's eyes hardened. Family. She used to have a family. But Smythe and his three buddies had destroyed that. They'd all pay for what they'd done to her father.

Weeks later, the *Indy Tattler* scandal sheet announced the upcoming divorce of Jeffrey and Gloria Smythe and his unexpected resignation from his own company's board. Lena pumped her fist in the air and celebrated with a freshly squeezed mimosa.

One down. Three to go.

#

Next up was Stanley Pendergast, the odd duck on her list. The youngest. No wife or kids. A runner and strict vegetarian. Squeaky clean. He'd be a challenge.

It may take months, but I'll get you. I'll hit you where it hurts.

Then she got lucky. She tailed Pendergast to the Polka Dot Pony, one of his favorite spots, and was observing him when her waitress, Penny according to her nametag, noticed her checking him out.

"Don't set your sights on him, honey," she said, nodding in Pendergast's direction. "Not unless you're into kinky sex."

Lena glanced at the seemingly straight-as-an-arrow guy. "You've got to be kidding. What makes you say that?"

"I've been to his place. Me and my kid sister." The waitress, who looked to be all of eighteen, shuddered. "He's got one whole room dedicated to sex toys. Like that show—*50 Shades of Grey*."

Lena's Spidey sense kicked in. "What happened? He didn't do anything to you, did he?"

"The bastard came on to Annie, my kid sister. She's fifteen but looks younger. He showed us his collection of whips and bondage stuff. He was as proud of them as if they were jewels from King Tut's tomb. When he told Annie how beautiful she was and ran his hands down her face, I nearly punched him."

"How can you stand to wait on him?"

"He may be a perv but he's a good tipper, and I'm working my way through school. Can't afford to piss off someone like him. Fortunately, I didn't have to. Two schoolgirls came over. While he was occupied with them, I grabbed Annie and left."

"Have you been back since then?"

"Naw." She smiled, then turned somber. "And I don't let Annie come around here anymore."

Lena paid, leaving Penny a hefty tip. She avoided looking at Pendergast as she left. If she'd made eye contact, she would have confronted the twisted son-of-a-bitch with more than a verbal assault. She'd been waiting years to make Smythe, Pendergast, Maxwell and Alistair Simmonds pay. She wasn't going to put them on their guard now. With a little unorthodox assistance from her, the police would soon have Pendergast off the streets.

It took Lena a month of surveillance to capture camera shots of the young girls who entered and exited his home. She even found a few names to go with the pictures, thanks to the nearby high school's Facebook page. She also included the name of the helpful waitress at the Polka Dot Pony. Finally, she had enough on Pendergast to ensure the IMPD would be interested enough to dig deeper into his activities.

Lena pulled on a pair of nitrate gloves and placed the evidence in a plain manila folder along with the letter she'd written giving Pendergast's name, address, and the significance of the young women she'd named. A short black wig, oversized sunglasses, and a Colts baseball cap transformed her into a delivery service carrier so she could drop off the evidence at the nearest police station.

It took another month before Lena had the satisfaction of seeing Pendergast being handcuffed and arrested on the evening news. It was worth the wait. Where he was going, he wouldn't prey on underage girls for a long time.

Two down. Two to go.

#

Sex wasn't an option for bringing down Kevin Maxwell, her third target. She found no hint that he enjoyed sex with women, men, kids, or aliens. Lena wondered how he and his wife, Debbie, had managed to produce the requisite two blond, blue-eyed brats. Most weekdays, Maxwell was at the office or in meetings from seven in the morning until nine at night. Weekends, he spent at his country club, either on the golf course or conducting informal business meetings in the club's private meeting rooms. He lived for his business. And that's where she'd hurt him.

Lena tapped her fingernails on the table. What she needed was an insider. Maxwell may be impervious to feminine wiles, but he had a young assistant. George something. He struck her as being eager to please and malleable. She probably wouldn't even have to have sex with him to procure enough information to plot Maxwell's downfall.

The next day, Lena waited outside the Starbucks where she knew George grabbed a coffee and a slice of lemon cake each morning, and followed him in.

"Oh, excuse me," she said after "accidentally" bumping into George and splashing coffee on his suit. "I'm so sorry." She took his coffee, cake, and messenger bag and set them down on a table, then grabbed a handful of napkins and dabbed at his jacket. She was as touchy-feely as she could be without overdoing it. "There, I think that will do." She stuck out her hand and grabbed his in hers. "I'm Melodie Gillam, by the way."

He blushed redder than a Christmas Poinsettia. "I'm, I'm George. George Moore," he said, retrieving his things. "Thank you, for, uh, you know, cleaning my jacket."

"Nice to meet you, George. You come here often?"

George shifted his weight from one leg to the other and grabbed his coffee as though he thought it might fly away. "Um, yeah. Every morning about this time."

She laid on her Southern accent. "Well, maybe I'll run into y'all later. I just moved here from Loo-a-vul. Sure would help if I knew someone who could show me around, but unfortunately, I don't know a soul in Indianapolis." She looked up at him with big baby blues, courtesy of Walmart Optical.

"Um, I'd be happy to help." He reached into his pocket. "I have to dash to the office, but here's my card. Give me a call if you want to go to lunch or if you have any questions or, um, anything."

"Thank you, George. I sure will."

She'd call him on Friday. Meanwhile, she'd dig deeper into the businesses and people connected to Maxwell. It was amazing how much dirt you could pick up from wait staff and supposed "friends." She'd put on her black wig, Tory Burch country-club attire, Reva ballet flats, and her diamond tennis bracelet and hang out at the country club as Maxwell's guest. No one would question her as long as she dressed the part—and Maxwell didn't show up.

#

George was Mr. Information Central. He was lonely and unsure of himself: a baby in the cutthroat corporate world. She almost felt remorse at using him. Almost. Within a few weeks he felt comfortable enough to ask her opinion on work documents he'd brought home. It was against the rules, but George felt like he had to work overtime to meet Maxwell's expectations.

"Melodie" lied and told him she had an MBA. Not exactly true. No college degree of any kind was hanging on Lena's office wall. But George jumped on that lie like he couldn't believe his good luck. Lena assisted him several nights a week and weekends. Before long, she procured the names of the acquisitions Maxwell was working on and the people involved.

Once, after she sent George to pick up a bottle of wine, she'd photographed all the documents in his messenger bag, including work passwords from his moleskin notebook. She'd bet her diamond bracelet that the Department of Justice and Federal Trade Commission would be interested in her findings and start an investigation. She'd also send copies to the companies he planned to swindle. Even if the DOJ and FTC didn't bite, word-of-mouth alone would bring him down. Maxwell's business reputation wouldn't be worth diddly-squat. George might become collateral damage, but it was all for the higher good.

Three down. One to go. The big fish. Alistair.

#

Before she went after Alistair, Lena needed cash, and lots of it. She made a quick call and set up the meeting. From Alistair, she'd learned the power of collecting secrets. It was a good gig when she needed quick money or favors. She was exceptionally good at it. She had but one unbreakable rule: Her target had to be a total scumbag, someone who'd used their influence to harm others who didn't deserve it.

She smoothed her black wig, secured the clasp on her diamond bracelet, and slipped her Sig Sauer P238 into a custom Italian leather concealed carry purse.

Within fifteen minutes, she arrived at Metamorphosis, a dimly lit, exclusive bar where a couple could engage in private conversation—a divorce settlement, blackmail, murder for hire, political intrigue. It was one of Indy's best kept secrets.

The Metamorphosis staff knew Lena as Sissie Summerton. "Sissie" was a big tipper and easy to satisfy, which made her a favorite. Of course, they likely assumed she was a high-priced call girl. She didn't discourage their misconception. Who knows when it might come in handy?

She arrived early and secured a secluded booth near the back of the bar, then ordered for two. A gin and tonic with a lime twist, hold the gin, for her. A bourbon straight up for her "client," Jim Bascomb. Minutes later, he swooped in and stomped over to the booth like a coach dressing down a referee who'd just fouled out the team's basketball star.

"What guarantee do I have that you won't sell my private business to the highest bidder?" he asked as he slid into the booth across from her.

Lena hid her look of disgust. Like he'd given guarantees to the hundreds of people he'd scammed.

"You have my word, Mr. —"

"Stop!" he hissed, leaning toward her and gripping the edge of the table. "Don't name me." He looked over his shoulder and back again. "This place could be bugged."

Lena traced the rim of her glass with the forefinger of her right hand and waited until Bascomb settled back in the booth. "As I said, you have my word."

"I need to think this over." He mopped his brow with an embroidered handkerchief.

Lena sat up taller and clasped both hands in front of her. "What's to think over? You really have no choice, do you?" She stopped to let that sink in. "Give me my asking price and we've got a deal." She hoped this did the trick. She had other business to attend to. She was meeting Alistair's former personal assistant for drinks and dinner at The Trader, her favorite hangout. If all went well, the scoop on Alistair would be served up with a slice of The Trader's flourless chocolate cake.

"But how do I know I can trust you?" His whine was pathetic.

Lena smiled. "You'll have to have a little faith." She had him right where she wanted him. Too bad she didn't have time to make him squirm more. "Now, do we have a deal? I'm not going to ask again." Lena sat back and stared Bascomb in the eyes. She began mentally counting backwards from one hundred. He broke contact at ninety-four.

"You'd better not double-cross me," he said as he pulled his cellphone from his pocket and accessed his bank app. "Where do I transfer the funds?"

#

Later that evening, Lena shed her clothes, poured bubble bath into the oversized soaking tub, and filled it with water. She liked it hot as she could stand it. By the time the water cooled, the kinks from her muscles were usually gone, along with anything else that troubled her. But not tonight. Funny, since she'd learned useful tidbits about Alistair thanks to his recently fired personal assistant.

It was the other person she'd "met" that night that concerned her. During the first course, the "tingle," her built-in warning bell, traveled from the nape of her neck to her scalp. Someone was scrutinizing her. She felt as though a laser was stripping the flesh from her body to peer inside and see what made her tick. She was drawn to that person like a lost ship to a lighthouse beam.

She found him and their eyes locked. It was no one she recognized. He raised his glass to her, then stood, turned his back to her, and left. He moved with a dancer's grace, possessed the arrogance of a man who wasn't used to losing, and looked like a young Pierce Brosnan.

A minute later, a waitress handed her a business card with a name, Grant Taylor, and number on one side and a message on the other: 'Meet me here in the bar tomorrow at five for drinks. I have a proposition for you.'

Lena shivered and pulled the pashmina shawl close around her silk sleep shorts and top. The games she played weren't for sissies—even though that was one of her aliases. Every time she convinced a target to part with money or information, she put herself in danger. She carried her gun on all her assignations. Though she'd never used it, if her record at the firing range was any indication, she could hit any mark straight between the eyes.

She slipped into bed, but her thoughts circled back to the handsome stranger. Seduction wasn't his motive. Of that, she was sure. It was too much of a coincidence that she met him so soon after taking down her third target. Who was he? Had Alistair figured out her game plan and sent Grant Taylor as a warning? What did he know about her other than she hung out at The Trader? And how? Had he been spying on her?

Lena shook her head, then rolled on her side. She was as paranoid as that weasel Bascomb. The last few months had been brutal. After she brought Alistair down, she was going to take an extended vacation. The brochures showcased the Maldives' bewitchingly beautiful beaches. The Maldives also featured an additional attraction: No extradition treaty with the U.S.

#

Lena dressed with care for her meeting at The Trader. Nothing too sexy. Nothing sexless either. A classic look—black pants paired with an off-the-shoulder white silk top—won out. She wore black ballet slippers for a quick get-away if needed, and her concealed carry purse. She was set.

She wished she knew more about Grant Taylor, but a search had netted her nothing. It was probably an alias. Well, two could play that game. Tonight, she'd be "Sissie."

Her plan was to beat him there and select the table, but when she arrived at half past four, he waved at her, then stood as she approached. He had already ordered, and she was barely seated before the waiter set their drinks in front of them.

He held his drink up to clink glasses. "Nice to meet you in the flesh, Lena Langtree."

Lena's mouth went dry and she took a big gulp from her G&T. This one came with gin, thank goodness. She didn't say anything immediately. Just stared at him. "You must be mistaken," she finally said. "My name's Sissie."

He smiled at her as if he'd caught her snitching cookies out of the cookie jar. "That's not what my intel says. Now, I'm not adverse to playing footsie with a beautiful woman. But I think we both have better things to do. Am I right?"

Lena pursed her lips and crossed her ankles, willing her legs not to fidget. She wasn't liking this conversation one bit. *Keep your cool. He'll let his guard down at some point. When he does, pounce.*

"I thought so. I have three little words for you. Smythe. Pendergast. Maxwell."

Lena sat back as if she didn't have a care in the world and smiled. "Are you sure you wouldn't rather play footsie?" She dropped one slipper and ran her foot up the inside of his leg stopping just short of his groin. Her smile was as wicked as his was amused.

He shifted his weight from one hip to another. "As enjoyable as I suspect that would be, I think we'd better stick to business for now."

"Who do you work for?" Lena blurted out.

"Let's just say I'm with a government agency. One that's interested in taking down the same people you seem to have a vested interest in. Smythe. Pendergast. Maxwell. And would it be a stretch to add Alistair Simmonds to the list?"

"These names mean nothing to me," Lena said, taking a deep breath and letting it out slowly.

"Oh, I think they do. Let's see if this refreshes your memory. These four men once owned the controlling stock in a pharmaceutical company. About a decade ago, they figured they'd make big bucks selling performance-enhancing drugs to racehorse trainers and owners at major racetracks and betting on the enhanced horses at the races. If successful, they'd go bigger, working their way up to the international racetracks. Simmonds buddied up to your father, the chief racing steward at Louisville's Horse Racing Commission, hoping to pull him into the scheme. But your father couldn't be bribed. He investigated rumors about doping and other unsavory practices. He kept them at bay and cost them a bundle of money. At least until a smear campaign they funded ousted him from office." He paused. "That about cover it?"

Lena remained mute, her face a mask of indifference. *Where in the hell did he dig up all this?*

Grant sat up straight, steepled his hands on the table and held her gaze. "Recently, someone virtually destroyed the lives of Smythe, Pendergast, and Maxwell."

"What's that got to do with me?"

"I think you were the one that set everything in motion. In fact, I have proof you did." He reached into his jacket pocket and pulled out three photos, spreading them on the table. "Here you are at the JW Marriott with Smythe." He pointed to the next one. "Here you are leaving the police department after dropping off the goods on Pendergast. And there's you making palsies with Maxwell's assistant. A little young for you, isn't he?"

Lena raised one eyebrow and took a sip of her drink before replying. "So, what is it you want?"

"We figure you're going after Simmonds next. Right?"

Lena shrugged her shoulders.

"Stop. We're looking into him. He's involved in a shitload of shady deals nationwide—drugs, prostitution, gambling. We'll handle him."

"And if I refuse?"

He retrieved a fourth photo from his pocket and threw it on the table. It was her with Bascomb. "You keep away from Simmonds and we'll overlook this. If you continue being a one-woman vigilante, we'll charge you with extortion. Your choice."

Lena looked down at the table, then back up at him, eyes wide. "I guess you've got me. Okay. We'll do it your way. Just promise me he'll be arrested."

"I can guarantee it."

Lena settled back in her chair. "Tell me, how did you find out what I was doing?"

"You know I can't reveal my sources." Grant grinned, appearing totally at ease now he thought he had her under control.

Like she could be controlled.

"I see." It was Lena's turn to steeple her hands on the table. "So, how do I know you won't charge me with extortion, anyway?"

"You don't. You'll just have to trust me."

Lena didn't like it when the table was turned on her. She wanted to smack that smug smile off his face.

"Now our business is concluded, how about another drink followed by dinner? And perhaps we can go from there . . .?"

One side of Lena's mouth turned up and she shook her head. "Sorry. I never mix business with pleasure." She stood up and slowly sauntered away, swaying her hips to taunt him.

#

Lena paced from one end of her bedroom to the other. Alistair and his friends had cost her father his job, reputation, and financial security. But Alistair went further. Taylor didn't know the half of it.

She'd been fifteen when Alistair had robbed her of her virginity. She thought the first time would be the last. Instead, Alistair offered her an internship at his company's Fortune 100 headquarters. Her father thought Alistair was a friend and he urged her to accept—grateful for the opportunity that would surely guarantee her acceptance to a top college. He was so proud when Alistair presented her with her own key to the corporate headquarters on a blue ribbon to be worn around her neck.

Lena clenched her fists. She never told her father about the sexual abuse. He had a bad heart and since he was her only surviving parent, she wasn't taking any chances with his health.

Lena's "job" consisted of working in Alistair's "private conference room" in the bowels of the building. The official story was that she was there to reorganize the files in the cabinets that lined the conference room walls. In reality, she didn't file a damn thing. She was there to be Alistair's plaything.

He taught her plenty, but nothing she could put on a college application. When he was done with her, he'd laugh, pat her on the head or the behind, and call her his "good girl." Lena could have blocked out everything and retreated into herself. Instead, she listened to everything her tormentor said: learned how he conducted business, read the files, discovered his secrets.

Lena swiped at the tear that trickled down her right cheek. She was tough, then and now. Then, she focused on the future rather than what was happening to her in the present. But when her father refused to capitulate to the group's demands, Alistair, who knew about her father's heart condition, sent him a video. The last thing her father saw before he died was Alistair perpetrating vile sex acts on his fifteen-year-old daughter. She hated Alistair for what he had done to her. But she hated him even more for causing her father's death.

Alistair would pay. By her hand. Not the FBI's.

Lena slapped her thighs as she paced, as if that would sharpen her thinking. What was it Alistair's ex-personal assistant had said? She'd blabbed on and on about how cheap he was. How he wouldn't pony up to help her with childcare but saw nothing ironic about building a luxurious personal spa in the headquarters basement complete with meditation room, lap pool, Swiss shower, and sauna. It would be finished this coming Monday. Alistair had asked her to hold all his appointments that morning because he was going to start his day with a session in the sauna. Solo.

"I hope he drowns in that fancy-schmancy pool of his," she'd said as she'd knocked down her third margarita. "Would serve him right."

Lena unlocked her closet safe and retrieved a key on a blue ribbon, holding it straight in front of her so she'd have as little contact with it as possible. How ironic that the item that represented her bondage that summer could be her means to getting justice over Alistair.

#

On Sunday, Lena conducted a trial run to see if her key would work. It did. No one had thought to upgrade to a passcard. Alistair would be alone and vulnerable. Just where she wanted him. She'd also swiped a housekeeper's uniform that should make accessing the building easier.

Early Monday morning, she donned a short blond wig, the uniform, an olive anorak jacket, Keds, and sunglasses. She packed her bags and tossed them in the SUV she'd "borrowed" from a neighbor who was out of town. Finally, she stashed her gun, equipped with a silencer, a pair of gloves, iPad, airplane ticket, and cash into her purse.

Showtime.

Lena hoped security would buy her story about it being her first day on the job and she wanted to arrive early to make a good impression. When she saw Sean Einhaus at the desk, she smiled. He'd worked there the summer she had. He was better known for his laziness than his intellect. He didn't bother with any paperwork. Just waved her on.

She took the elevator to the basement and tamped down the queasy feeling in her stomach she'd experienced as a scared fifteen-year-old. She drew herself up to her full height, swallowed hard, and headed to her hiding spot in the spa.

She didn't have long to wait. Right on cue, Alistair dropped trou and stepped inside the sauna. Straight into the sights of her gun.

"Hi, Alistair."

"What is this? A joke?"

The asshole didn't seem in the slightest bit afraid or upset. Didn't even try to hide his manhood.

"No joke." She pulled off the wig and shook out her hair.

"Lena?" This time his voice wavered.

Lena smiled but her eyes glowed like embers. "I'm surprised you remember me as anything other than your 'good girl.' Well, your 'good girl' is all grown up." She tossed a pair of handcuffs on the bench behind him. "Now be a 'good boy' and put those on."

"Lena, please. I'm sorry for what I did. It was wrong. I know that. Let me make it up to you. Let's go to my office and I'll write you a check."

She moved toward him and jabbed her gun into his ribs. He fastened the cuffs.

"I don't think you understand. I don't want your money."

She pointed the gun at his head and pulled the trigger.

Right between the eyes. That's for you, Dad.

As Lena drove to the airport, she contemplated what she'd done. Would her father approve? Or would he think she was no better than Alistair? She liked to think of herself as an avenging angel. A true good girl. But maybe she was making excuses for what she'd become.

Perhaps she'd find her answer when she felt the warm sand between her toes as she walked along those beaches in the Maldives.

About the author

Shari Held is an Indianapolis-based, award-winning fiction author who spins tales of mystery, horror, and romance. Her short stories have been published in numerous magazines and anthologies, including *Hoosier Noir 3, Yellow Mama, Homicide for the Holidays, Asinine Assassins*, and *Murder 20/20*, for which she served as co-editor.

Veronica Leigh
STRANGE FRUIT

September 1932

Ouabache, Indiana

Sheriff Claire Williams produced a hanky from her pocket and held it over her nose and mouth. She hesitantly approached the young black man who was swinging by his neck from the maple tree. Dear God in heaven! Deputy Frank and dozens of men and women stood off to the side, gawking, unfazed by the horrific sight. What remained of the boy's face was disfigured: nose and lips dangling off by threads of skin, eyeballs gouged out and lying on the ground. He was like a piece of strange fruit, mottled by abuse, over-ripened by the rising sun, and swarmed by buzzing flies. The stench of decay in the humid valley air soured her stomach and indicated he had been lynched hours ago. And I was neglected to be notified.

Deputy Frank was speaking to the growing crowd, swapping stories and cracking jokes. They were on the outskirts of Ouabache, on a piece of land used for the church revival earlier that summer. By word of mouth, a rumor spread through Ouabache that a young black man had been strung up. And that was how Claire first heard of it, in the grocery store. While she was the sheriff and should have been aware of such a travesty, she slept soundly during the lynching the night before, none the wiser.

Claire stalked over to the deputy, grabbed his elbow, and dragged him from his audience. "Why was I not immediately informed of this?" She removed the hanky from her face and spoke through grit teeth. She didn't care about embarrassing the deputy in front of the eavesdropping spectators.

Deputy Frank's weaselly face reddened and he frowned. "Well, uh, I thought—"

"I don't care what you thought, deputy." Claire interrupted. "I'm the sheriff of Ouabache and from this point on, you will inform me of all crimes in this area. Is that understood?"

"Yes...sheriff." The deputy grumbled.

Claire was well-aware of the disdain he had for her and the small bit of power she wielded. Deputy Frank had expected to assume the position of sheriff, after her husband Reginald died. The commissioner had selected her, to fill her husband's shoes, and the deputy balked at taking orders from a woman. Widow's Succession. The commissioner called it. Occasionally, when a politician or sheriff died, the widow of the man assumed his position and served the remainder of his term. Were it not for the commissioner's gentle persuasion and being on hard times, she never would have accepted it. Deputy Frank, on the other hand, resented that she was chosen to wear the sheriff's badge rather than he. Nothing would change overnight, but it had been a month since she had been sworn-in and she hoped to have made a little progress. However, Deputy Frank went out of his way to undermine her.

He'll never view me as anything more than the little homemaker who stole his job. Claire returned to the corpse, craning her neck back to look at him.

"Who is our victim?" She lifted her hand, gesturing to the body. A thick, south wind stirred and once more she placed the hanky over her nose. She left her mouth bare so she could speak, but it allowed her to taste death in the air.

The black population of Ouabache was small and with a little deduction, if the boy had his face, she would have known him by his surname at least.

"Bucky Thomson." Deputy Frank spat the name of the deceased out like a curse word. "He raped the reverend's daughter a few months ago and confessed. I imagine this is retribution. Folks probably couldn't stand hearing that his sentence was changed to life in prison."

One could not live in Ouabache and not know of the tragedy of Alice Gibson. When her husband arrested Bucky Thomson, he was hailed a hero. There was little investigation, the whole thing was finished within 48 hours. Good triumphed over evil and no one questioned the outcome. Bucky was black, ergo he was guilty as sin. Alice Gibson would be vindicated and Bucky Thomson would likely receive the death penalty. Reginald died not long after, and Claire had been so wrapped up in her own grief and new occupation, she hadn't paid any mind to the latest gossip.

"So, a mob took Bucky Thomson out of his prison cell?" Claire glared at the deputy, waiting for the paltry explanation he would offer up. Reginald had thought Deputy Frank was shifty, and she suspected him of being corrupt. She supposed that was why the commissioner chose her to be sheriff rather than the deputy. However, she didn't have any evidence of questionable actions. "Where were the guards?"

Deputy Frank hemmed and hawed before responding, "The guards must have been overpowered. They—the mob was huge."

She returned her attention to Bucky and grimaced. Along with the smell of rot, he smelled burnt, a sign he had been set on fire. His clothing was torn in several places, shoes pitched to the side, and fingers and toes were missing. Folks liked to claim souvenirs of the lynched. It wouldn't be long before many households owned a piece of clothing or a body part of Bucky Thomson.

A flash of light from behind made her jump. She turned and her whole body burned with rage as a photographer snapped pictures of the deceased. No respect for the dead. Soon photographs of the lynching would end up on postcards. Growing up, she heard stories about the black man lynched off the Wabash River bridge...her father had a picture postcard of the lynching.

Claire shoved the hanky back into her skirt pocket. "Get out of here!" She shouted, but her voice was drowned out by a sorrowful wail.

"Bucky!" A lone woman's cries rang throughout the valley and the crowd parted as a black woman dashed up to the tree. "No!" She wrapped her arms around Bucky's deformed feet, clinging to them. "He didn't do it. He didn't rape that girl!"

The woman needed no introduction. Claire knew from the second the woman let out that howl, she was Bucky Thomson's mother. The woman's weeping had no effect on the crowd. They were still snapping photographs, chatting, and now singing broke out.

Claire dared to lay a hand on the woman's shoulder and regretted it when the woman jerked away. "Mrs. Thomson?" she whispered, hating to cause this poor mother further pain. "Will you come with me to the sheriff's office?"

Mrs. Thomson nodded.

Claire stepped away from the body and Mrs. Thomson and moved towards the deputy. Deputy Frank had resumed regaling the crowd with stories, coaxing ripples of laughter out of them. She was filled with a burning desire to slap the man. But unlike Frank, one step out of line would cost her this job. Then Bucky's murder would be swept under the rug.

She wedged herself between the deputy and the crowd. "Get these people out of here." He bristled. Disregarding his displeasure, she jabbed a finger into his chest. "And you cut him down and take him to Jed Loving. Be respectful about it." Lowering her tone, she said, "I'll know if there's any further maltreatment. Jed will tell me."

Deputy Frank began to dismiss the crowd and Claire was about to escort Mrs. Thomson to the sheriff's office, when she saw a bit of white standing out among the tree roots.

Reminding her of a flapping bird's wing, she believed it was a dove and almost shrugged it off. Until she saw it was a bit of pure white cloth. She crouched down and looking at it, it didn't match up with what remained of Bucky's clothing.

A clue, perhaps? Claire snatched it up, and linking arms with the deceased's mother, she led the grieving woman to her Model A.

#

Claire placed the steaming cup of tea in front of Mrs. Thomson, and then sat down behind the desk, opposite of the woman. The stove in the rear of the building wasn't good for much more than a warm drink, and she hoped this would suffice. The victim's mother curled her rough-hewn hands around the cup and inhaled the vapors. This gave Claire the opportunity to study the woman.

She isn't as old as I thought. Claire surmised, observing Mrs. Thomson as she sipped the brew. She can't be more than a few years older than me. Her features were currently not contorted by grief, and though she had a few wrinkles around the eyes and mouth, Mrs. Thomson carried a youthful vitality. Claire estimated the woman must have been young when she had Bucky. The burden this woman would carry for the rest of her life, the way her son died, was more than anyone should carry alone.

Claire glanced at the silent telephone and was surprised to have not yet received word from Dr. Jed Loving. Then again, perhaps the condition of the body made it more difficult to conduct the autopsy.

"He didn't do it." Mrs. Thomson stated abruptly, slamming the teacup down on the desk. It was a wonder it didn't shatter. "Bucky didn't do it."

Claire nodded. "Tell me about your son." She prodded gently as she could.

Mrs. Thomson's mouth twisted. "Bucky...Buchanan was my pride and joy." She dragged her left palm across her cheeks, rubbing them dry. "My husband left when Bucky was ten and though I told him he didn't have to, he became the man of the house. Bucky was book smart. He was saving up for college. He was going to make something of himself."

The woman continued, voice swelled with pride, sharing anecdote after anecdote. Claire listened, nodding occasionally, and then she rose from her seat and went to the filing cabinet. She withdrew the case file of the rape of Alice Gibson and returned to the desk. Claire skimmed the documents, to get a better idea of what evidence had been collected and looked over Bucky Thomson's signed confession. The young man was quoted verbatim, describing how he had his eye on Alice for months and how he abducted and savagely molested her. From Claire's point of view, everything looked correct.

Yet, the Bucky Thomson described by his mother didn't match up with a soulless rapist.

"I have the case file here." Claire piped up, pressing her fingertips together, tenting her hands. "Bucky confessed to the crime."

"That was after hours of interrogation." Mrs. Thomson retorted. The pleasant expression, the one she sported while spinning yarns, faded and was replaced with a hardened one. "The sheriff and the deputy beat it out of my boy."

Claire shook her head, protesting, "No, my husband conducted the interrogation. He wouldn't have…" She fell silent when she received a withering look from Bucky's mother.

No matter what she said in Reginald's defense, Mrs. Thomson was convinced the lawmen had violently coerced the confession from Bucky. The woman, after all, didn't know Reginald…No, she met him at some point since he conducted the investigation.

But Reginald wasn't abusive. He never laid a finger on me. A memory trickled through her mind, from a few months ago, of Reginald coming home one evening after work, with bruised and bloody knuckles. They never said a word about the abrasions and they were quickly forgotten.

He wasn't prejudiced. Claire insisted to herself, despite reminisces of Reginald making the occasional joke about blacks and immigrants.

The deputy I can see beating Bucky, but Reginald? Though she would like to believe her husband innocent of any wrongdoing, Claire couldn't be so sure.

"What else could Bucky do?" Mrs. Thomson held her palms upwards and shrugged. "They wouldn't accept the truth and he couldn't handle the torture. He had to confess."

Claire felt her chest constrict. It was all she could do not to defend Reginald. Though it seemed like a personal attack, this wasn't about him. This was about Bucky and Alice Gibson.

"All right." Claire decided the best thing to do was to hear the woman out. "What is the truth then, Mrs. Thomson?"

Mrs. Thomson took a long drink of her tea, draining the cup. Once more she slammed it down on the desk, making Claire flinch. "That little harlot lied about my Bucky. She had a hankering for him, but he wanted nothing to do with her." She straightened her shoulders defiantly. "So, she cried rape and now my son is dead." Reaching across the desk and placing her hand on top of Claire's, voice shaking, "Please, my son didn't deserve to be treated like that."

Claire locked eyes with Mrs. Thomson and found herself agreeing with her. Bucky Thomson didn't deserve to be torn from his jail cell, mutilated, and hung. Especially if there was a chance he was innocent. If Reginald and Deputy Frank had beaten a confession out of Bucky, then in all likelihood the evidence and the reports were falsified.

I have to re-open the case. Claire turned her wrist and she pressed Mrs. Thomson's fingers. "I'll do what I can, Mrs. Thomson." She promised.

#

Claire sensed Deputy's Frank rage reverberating off of his taut frame as they followed Rev. Gibson into the parsonage parlor. She had given the deputy strict instructions to remain silent and take notes while she asked the questions. After his recent unprofessional behavior, she would have preferred him to stay at the sheriff's office. But a male presence would make Gibson more inclined to take the investigation seriously.

Rev. Gibson motioned for them to sit on the sofa, opposite of him. Despite the fact the sheriff's star was pinned to her, his attention was focused on Deputy Frank.

Claire laced her fingers and demurely laid them in her lap. "I'm sure by now you've heard of the lynching of Bucky Thomson." She didn't bother to hide her smirk when the reverend's head snapped up.

She ought to be used to men overlooking her, however, it still stung. On the other hand, she could use their underestimation to her advantage. Their eyes were never on her, she could slip behind the scenes more easily than a man; questions could roll off her tongue and stun whoever she queried.

"God works in mysterious ways." Gibson's nose and mustachioed upper lip twitched. That peculiar tick of his often distracted Claire during his fire and brimstone sermons. One day she counted thirty-seven twitches throughout the sermon. "Only He could remove such evil from this world."

"Amen." Deputy Frank put in, withdrawing a notepad from his trouser pocket.

Claire counted to ten. If she lost her temper before the reverend, she would be the one to appear ridiculous. "Keep your comments to yourself, deputy," she scolded. "I'd like to speak to your daughter, reverend. It's pertinent to the investigation."

Rev. Gibson's gaze darted from her, to the deputy, and back again. At first, he didn't respond and Claire wasn't surprised. The man often preached how a woman's place was in the home. A woman in authority, such as she, unnerved him.

"Alice has a delicate constitution." Rev. Gibson finally answered, taking a handkerchief to mop his sweaty forehead. "This has upset her greatly."

"Be that as it may, I must speak to her." Claire insisted.

There was a thud from the floor above and the pitter-patter of dainty feet on the stairs that led into the foyer. Someone is listening. The parsonage had thin walls, and voices echoed throughout the large, airy rooms.

A slight girl in a child-like frock slipped into the parlor and was trembling as she stood before Claire and the deputy. Not exactly the harlot Mrs. Thomson described. Though she had seen the minister's daughter in church and at other functions, she didn't know Alice Gibson well. Since her mother's death a few years prior, she was a shadowy creature who seemed to vanish in public even when physically present.

Alice looked on the verge of fainting. Claire hated to question the girl, but there was no way around it. "Miss Gibson, I'll try not to take up too much of your time or cause you too much trouble." She kept her tone gentle as she spoke. "Bucky Thomson was murdered last night. He was lynched last night. I spoke to his mother this morning and she believed him innocent of your rape accusation."

Alice let out a noise, akin to the cry of a wounded animal.

Rev. Gibson slammed a fist on the coffee table, causing both Claire and Alice to jerk. "How dare she— how dare that…" He didn't say the word, but he might as well have. It hung over their heads, like an ominous cloud. "…woman question the truth!"

Deputy Frank grunted, but kept scribbling in his notepad.

Claire disregarded the men and focused on the girl. "Miss Gibson, could you tell me what happened between you and Bucky?"

"I…" A lone tear slid down Alice's thin face. "Bucky wouldn't leave me alone, he followed me everywhere, calling me names. Then on my way home from school one day, he kidnapped me, took me to the woods, and he took advantage of me." The girl hunched her shoulders and made herself appear smaller than what she was. "I thought I was going to die. Daddy found me, he saved me."

Claire watched her carefully and sighed. She detected truth in all of Alice's looks and behavior and the story seemed plausible. Since the beginning of time, girls had been victims of men and boys and had to suffer in silence. Often enough, such things were covered up by families of both the victim and the abuser. The only reason this was brought to light was because of Bucky's race.

What is the truth? Claire pondered. There were a dozen possibilities and any of them could be true. That Alice was being honest, that Bucky had abducted and raped her. Or perhaps Mrs. Thomson was right about Alice Gibson.

Whatever the truth, Bucky was murdered as a result. Lord knows the reverend had a motive as well. Any father would want to kill the man who raped his daughter. Even without that, Rev. Gibson's temper and his prejudice against Bucky would have been reason enough.

Claire handed Alice a hanky and her heart twisted as the girl hid her face in the material. "I see. Thank you for your honesty." She thought of patting the girl's shoulder but stopped, not wanting to make Alice any more uncomfortable. "I won't trouble you any further. You'll be in my prayers."

Deputy Frank closed the notebook and slid it back into his pocket. He shook his head and muttered the previously unspoken, ominous word.

Claire was on the way to the door, but didn't miss Alice flinching when the girl heard that word. The word clearly bothered Alice in a way it didn't bother her father.

Nor did she miss the conspicuous, little nods the deputy and the reverend exchanged. They could have been politely saying good-bye, but when Claire noticed how they saluted one another by holding up three fingers, there was no denying a secret connection. She recalled that when the Ku Klux Klan ran rampant in Indiana the previous decade, members would openly gesture to one another like that.

#

Claire asked the Lord for strength to not lose her temper as she entered the doctor's office. Jed Loving had Bucky Thomson's body for over a day and he still hadn't telephoned her. Her own telephone calls to him went unanswered, and he didn't come into the sheriff's office to speak to her. It's not like him.

She stormed to the examination room reserved for autopsies. The pungent stench of death and rotting flesh slammed into her and right away her eyes caught Bucky's lifeless form on the table. A white sheet was draped over his naked body, drawn up to his chin, but his mottled face remained visible.

The room was unlit, the curtains drawn and silent as the grave. It took her a minute for her eyes to adjust to the dark, but when they did, she found the doctor slumped against the corner supply cabinet.

"Jed! Where have you been?" Claire went to the window and parted the curtains.

The sunlight drained in, casting a yellow beam on Jed. His hair was mussed, his blood splattered clothing disheveled, and an empty bottle of likely illegal hooch was lying nearby.

"Are you all right?" Claire counted to ten and pinched the bridge of her nose. The last thing she needed was Ouabache's sole doctor getting sick or dying of alcohol poisoning.

"No." Jed harrumphed, and using his shirt sleeve, he mopped his face. "My report is on the counter." He gestured to the paperwork laying above his head.

Claire snatched it up and skimmed it, choking on the bile climbing the back of her throat. "My God."

Jed shoved the bottle away and pushed himself to his feet. "I've treated my share of patients and done my share of autopsies, but this..." He pointed to Bucky, his voice cracking under the weight of emotion, "You wouldn't think men capable of this. Sheriff Williams, they beat him, burned him, cut off his manhood, and that was all before the lynching. Our neighbors, our friends did this, folks we go to church with."

"This is nothing new." Claire averted her eyes, unable to look at Bucky. Somehow knowing precisely what the murderers did, made the condition of the body worse. That someone endured such cruelty, such hatred, before succumbing to death, convicted her. "Ten years ago, the Klan was thriving around here."

She never could reconcile how church-going folks could embrace the KKK, an organization based in hatred. Yet the previous decade, Hoosiers joined the Klan in droves, welcoming the group into their churches, burning crosses, and holding parades. She never joined, and as far as she knew, neither had Reginald. The most fervent kluxers seemed to be keen on racism and rabble-rousing, while others considered it a social group. After the Great War, everyone wanted to return to old-fashioned, family values and the KKK promised that.

"Yeah, I know, I was part of it." Jed sniffed, his nose and cheekbones pink from drink.

Claire covered her mouth. She shouldn't judge, but she did. Jed was a doctor, he wasn't uneducated or a fool, however, he too was swept up in the movement. It made her look at him in a different light. If a good, intelligent person could be seduced by hatred, anyone could.

"When Grand Dragon Stephenson was arrested for murder, I finally saw the light." Jed dropped his head, shaking it in shame. "But I spouted the same prejudices and overlooked other things."

"Are you saying you think the KKK did this to Bucky Thomson?" Claire heard herself ask. That would account for the piece of white cloth she found at the scene of the crime.

As a sheriff, it was one thing to confront racists. It was quite another thing to confront the KKK. After Stephenson's arrest, the KKK's membership dropped off and folks hid their white robes in their attics. But the organization itself was still able to cause trouble. If challenged, they could threaten her life.

"Not the official group itself, but former members, sure." Jed replied. "What made the Klan is still there, under the surface."

Claire drew in a deep breath and looked at Bucky. Or what was left of him. He didn't deserve this. No one did. If he were a white boy, he would have been left alone in prison. Or never would have been arrested altogether. Bucky deserved vindication.

"Was the reverend involved in the Klan?" she asked.

If Rev. Gibson had connections to the Klan, he could have easily rounded up enough cohorts to form a lynch party and hang Bucky.

"No. He never wanted anything to do with them. He refused to allow them to hold meetings in the church. Said they were God's scourge on Indiana."

Claire chewed her lower lip. Rev. Gibson might not be a member, but if he wanted to enact revenge on his daughter's alleged assailant, it wouldn't be a challenge to convince former Klan members to help.

Jed sniffed again and she detected a shiny glint on his cheek. Like most men, he did not show emotion in public and if she drew attention to it, he'd call it a droplet of sweat rolling down his cheek.

"Jed, you are not like the men who did this." Claire declared. Whatever his past mistakes, Jed was not a murderer. He wouldn't have done this; he would have drawn a line.

At least she hoped so. Their neighbors did not.

"No, I'm worse. I knew and did nothing to stop it." Jed countered and plucking the end of the sheet, he drew it over Bucky until the young man was fully concealed.

Mrs. Thomson's accusations, that Alice Gibson was a harlot and lied, rang in Claire's ears. And though it didn't ring true, she had to ask. "You examined Miss Gibson after the incident. Could she have been lying?" She couldn't let go of her doubts about Reginald and the case that landed Bucky into prison. No stone could go unturned. "Was the original report falsified?"

"I found evidence of Bucky's seed on her."

"I understand." Claire sighed. Nothing about this case made sense.

There was a girl who was raped and was a shell of her former self.

There was a dead young black man who had a promising future but committed a heinous crime.

There was a grieving mother convinced her son was an angel and the girl was evil.

There was the prejudiced reverend who scorned the Klan and believed the young black man to be the devil.

And now there was the KKK lurking in the shadows of this case, who would have loved nothing more than to avenge their cause. But there was no official Klan activity in the area.

Someone is lying. Claire knew she'd have to speak to all of the living witnesses once more.

#

That evening, Claire had already intended to call on Mrs. Thomson. But when she spotted a peculiar plume of grey smoke ascending into the twilight sky, beyond Ouabache, above where the woman lived, she drove over. Her deputy had been nowhere to be found, leaving her to venture out on her own. She floored the accelerator and cranked the steering wheel of her Model A Ford, turning the sharp corner of Dead Man's Curve. The unbricked, sloping road led past the area where the black families lived. If the KKK was being revived, or if former members were stirring up trouble, she suspected they were the cause of this particular fire. They could have set fire to Mrs. Thomson's house or...

Her suspicions were confirmed when her vehicle coasted to a stop and a burning cross stood in an empty field by the black residential area. The wood put off a powerful stench. Claire's eyes watered, a mix from the stench affecting her sinuses and tears. She hated seeing something so sacred be twisted like this.

"Yet man is born unto trouble, as the sparks fly upward." Claire murmured. Job 5:7. It was the verse Rev. Gibson used during Sunday's sermon.

A small crowd of black folks stood opposite of the cross, trembling, but they didn't leave. In her estimation, they were the bravest souls she had ever seen.

Mrs. Thomson emerged from the throng and paused within feet of the cross, placing her hands on her hips. She didn't bat an eyelash. The woman had lost her only son and was completely alone in the world. There was nothing left for her to lose.

As Claire drew near the site, her attention was drawn to one lone figure close to the foot of the cross. One swathed head to toe in white sheet. Unlike Mrs. Thomson who faced this anonymous fool head on, Claire quivered. She neither carried a gun, and her pair of handcuffs were in the glove compartment of the Model A Ford.

Jed had assured her that the Klan was not officially involved, yet here was a Klansman. Of short, slight build, the white sheet dwarfed the man, and her thoughts immediately went to Deputy Frank. He like many others in Ouabache, had a bone fragment of Bucky that he showed off; not to mention his comments during the interview with Alice Gibson.

Her spirits plummeted when she whipped the sheet off of the man's face and he was revealed to be the reverend. If it'd been the deputy, she could have arrested him and he would have lost his position. But the truth was often inconvenient and unpleasant.

Alas, Rev. Gibson straightened to his full height, puffing his chest out proudly.

Whilst several inches shorter, Claire clamped her hand down on the reverend's shoulder and spun him around. "Reverend Gibson, did you murder Bucky Thomson?" she asked.

He made no response, but she figured further investigation would prove he had been involved with the lynching. On closer inspection, she noticed a tear on his right arm sleeve and believed the bit of material found at the crime scene would match up with this robe. However, a plethora of questions remained. Jed had insisted that the reverend had not been a KKK member and opposed the organization. Was the reverend a secret member, or was he using the robe as a disguise to pin the blame on the group? He and Deputy Frank exchanged that three-finger salute…there was reason to believe the latter was involved.

The spectators toted water from the Wabash River and doused the massive cross. He would have needed help hoisting that up. There had to be others involved in this crime, as well as Bucky's murder.

"You're under arrest, Rev. Gibson." Claire said, and without any fuss, she propelled him in the direction of her car. Once she got the handcuffs out, she'd properly restrain him.

A chorus of cheers broke out and Claire felt a wave of satisfaction, for finally doing something right in regards to her job.

#

Claire slammed the door to the cell closed behind Rev. Gibson. She cringed at the shrill sound of the key turning in the lock. Withdrawing it, she slipped it into her skirt pocket and leveled her gaze at the man of God.

Reverend Gibson should have had the good graces to turn away. Instead, he looked her right in the eye, showing no shame for his sins. No shame for abducting a boy and lynching him, no shame for covering up his crime, and no shame for harassing the victim's mother and neighbors. She would interrogate him later, when her temper cooled, but she already knew he wouldn't be cooperative. With some work, she would prove him guilty. But unlike Bucky Thomson, he would do little time and after a while, the world would pardon him.

"There is a Judgment Day, reverend." Claire couldn't help reminding him. Before he could utter a retort, she left and took a short stroll to the sheriff's office.

Only Mrs. Thomson was present, sitting in the same chair she sat in the other morning. Deputy Frank had yet to rear his ugly head. Gibson likely wouldn't tell her if the deputy was involved in the lynching and cross burning, but observing the poor weeping mother, she vowed to bring him to justice too.

She sat down at her desk and was taking down the woman's account of all that had transpired that evening. Her fingers were beginning to cramp, and she sighed with relief when the front door opened.

Alice Gibson staggered into the building. Her blonde curls hung limply about her shoulders and her frock was mussed. There was a dark bruise beneath one of her eyes, one Claire was willing to wager had been made by her father's fist.

"Miss Gibson?" Claire rose to her feet and met the girl halfway, with Mrs. Thomson on her heels.

"Y-you arrested m-my D-daddy?" The girl sputtered.

Claire crossed her arms. "I have reason to believe Rev. Gibson killed Bucky Thomson."

Mrs. Thomson glowered at Alice, her hatred radiating of her. "Oh, he did it. There's no doubt in my mind." The woman insisted firmly, her jaw clenching. "My poor boy."

"This is my fault!" Alice exclaimed. Her eyes looked wild and Claire feared the girl was about to come unhinged.

"Why do you say that?" Claire waited and when the minister's daughter remained silent, she intoned the girl's name, "Alice?"

"I lied. Bucky didn't rape me." Alice dropped her head and hugged herself.

The room was silent enough Claire could hear a pin drop. One of the questions she had put to Jed Loving was if Alice had lied about the rape. However, Jed's findings proved otherwise.

"There was evidence that he did." Claire tried to swallow, but she felt as though she were choking.

The last thing she wanted to do was discuss such evidence in front of Bucky's mother. But Mrs. Thomson wasn't about offer them privacy. The woman had the girl pinned down under her incensed gaze.

Alice shook her head from side to side. "Bucky didn't take advantage of me. We loved each other." It occurred to Claire that this girl changed her story once before and whatever she was about to say must be taken with a grain of salt. The girl could be spinning another yarn just to save face. "He was my best friend and I loved him. We were going to get married when he was through with college." Sobs slurred her words. "One day, after school, Bucky and me ran off to the woods. We were...laying with one another. Daddy caught us together and he said he'd kill me and Bucky if I didn't say Bucky raped me. So, that's what I said."

Claire covered her mouth in astonishment. Of all the scenarios, I hadn't expected that. Alice and Bucky wouldn't have been the first youths to be intimate before wedlock. But in Indiana, for a white young lady and a black young man to consensually know each other in the Biblical sense, that went against all time-honored traditions. It makes sense. And the lie to hide their romantic relationship, was a last-ditch effort on the reverend's part.

A lie that escalated into murder. If Rev. Gibson hadn't tightened the noose around Bucky's neck and hung the young man himself —and she believed he had—he knew precisely who did. Lynching Bucky would send the truth to the grave with him.

And Reginald possibly knew all of this. Claire winced, she wanted to get sick. Her husband may have been good to her, and he was an upstanding,

Christian man in Ouabache. But he knew Bucky was innocent and he still coerced a confession from him.

Mrs. Thomson let out a wretched cry, similar to the one she let out when she found Bucky hanging from a tree. "You wicked, evil girl!" She screamed at the minister's daughter.

Before Claire could react and restrain her, Mrs. Thomson charged at Alice Gibson and slapped the girl across the face. The victim's mother seized the girl by the shoulders and violently shook her.

Claire snapped out of her stupor and pulled Mrs. Thomson off Alice, pushing her back towards the chair.

Mrs. Thomson dissolved into tears. It wasn't long before Alice collapsed in a heap on the floor and began to wail.

Claire stepped back and it occurred to her that Alice Gibson could be prosecuted for obstruction of justice. The girl's lie caused the death of an innocent young man. Then again, Rev. Gibson threatened to kill Alice if she didn't comply. The girl was a victim in her own way.

Unlike the first case she solved, this one's outcome couldn't be fixed. The reverend had been caught and he'd be tried, and hopefully his cohorts might eventually be revealed. But there would be no happy ending, not for Bucky Thomson, Mrs. Thomson, or Alice Gibson. Now her own perception of Reginald was altered; she didn't really know who he was anymore. But then again, this whole thing had shown her that she hadn't really known anyone at all.

About the author

Veronica Leigh has been published in seven nonfiction anthologies and was included in Sweetycat Press's "Who's Who of Emerging Writers 2021" anthology. Her essays have been featured on The Doe, 4W Publishing, and in Lumpen Journal. Her fiction has been published in Dark Moon Digest, After Dinner Conversation Magazine, ParAbnormal Magazine, NoSleep Podcast, Mystery Magazine, and Black Cat Mystery Magazine. She will eventually be published in Sherlock Holmes Mystery Magazine, Midnight of the Dying Garden Anthology, and Scare Street's Night Terrors anthology.

Brian Beatty

CHICAGO THAT ONE TIME

That time Hurley drove his truck up to Chicago for the giant swap meet at the biggest convention center in North America, he of course got caught in traffic on Lake Shore Drive.

But traffic wasn't the right word for it, because "traffic" suggests "travel" and Hurley lurched hardly more than two car lengths in an entire hour, and never saw a wreck or other reason why.

The big buyer-seller shindig went on without Hurley. He escaped from the start-stop parade onto the next exit ramp that came along. Which was how he wound up driving around lost on the city's far south side. What buildings didn't have plywood for windows had graffiti Hurley couldn't decipher tattooed across their crumbling bricks and mortar. He'd driven just seven hours, yet never felt so far from home.

Just in time he found a corner minimart that looked safe enough for a quick gas tank refill. He swiped his card at the pump praying a silent prayer that nobody would try to jump him.

"Indiana, huh? Where in Indiana?" a voice said, and Hurley turned. "Your license plates." The kid was wearing a loose, dirty college basketball uniform but would've had to balance on his tiptoes to stand six feet tall. He grinned a mouthful of fake gold teeth. "The hippie hollers of Indiana from the looks of you. What you got under there?" The teen nodded at Hurley's tie-dyed t-shirt and faded bib overalls, then the weatherproof tarp draped over the truck bed full of junk Hurley had hoped to rid himself of at the swap meet.

"Nothing that interesting, really."

"You don't know. I got pretty wild interests. So does my crew." This time he nodded toward a minivan full of other young guys snickering and slapping at each other.

Hurley shrugged. "I guess it wouldn't hurt to show you. A customer is a customer."

"That's what I been telling you, old man."

Hurley unhitched one corner of the tarp and reached inside. "These are popular," he said, throwing a cement frog the size a football at the kid's head before the kid could duck out of the way.

The kid and frog both landed on the mini-mart's asphalt lot with a thud. Only the frog bounced. The kid's gang banger buddies took a long moment to grasp what they'd just watched. By the time they came running to his defense, Hurley was in his truck grabbing the .38 he kept in his glove box. He fumbled getting the glove box open with shaking hands until it was almost too late.

"I've got bullets to go around," he shouted, his voice cracking. "Even if I miss a shot or two. Do the math." That slowed them down. "You should check on your pal. He went down pretty hard."

Nobody ran out of the minimart to rescue anybody or say they'd called 911 for the cops.

Hurley didn't actually keep the gun loaded, but the threat was enough to keep those thugs at a safe distance as he slowly replaced the gas pump handle and printed a receipt for tax reasons. If one made a move, Hurley just waved the gun around like he'd seen done on TV.

What those boys didn't know wouldn't hurt them.

Brian Beatty

WINNER WINNER

Hurley won the lottery. He didn't win the multi-million-dollar jackpot that makes the evening news when there aren't enough murders, weather emergencies, sports championships and car insurance commercials to fill the half-hour. He bought a winning scratch-off card worth a thousand dollars more than the convenience store cashier was allowed to pay out from her till.

That meant driving a hundred miles to lottery headquarters to collect his check in person. Then driving that same hundred miles back home, plus a trip to the bank. There would be taxes, too, Hurley was sure.

Fun wasn't worth it sometimes.

That day he took off from garage sale-ing to make the road trip to lottery headquarters, Hurley stopped first at the Blue Bonnet Café to treat himself to a fancy restaurant breakfast. Their biscuits and gravy weren't as delicious as his own, but they served theirs with bottomless glasses of freshly squeezed orange juice. And sparkling, striped vinyl booths gave the Blue Bonnet a time machine quality Hurley appreciated as a professional reseller of antiquarian kitsch.

"Well, hello, big winner. Everybody's saying your poor flea markets days are behind you," his server said with a wink.

"Don't believe everything you hear," Hurley replied.

"What are you planning then?"

"New overalls. Or maybe a new hat. Waiting to see what's left after Uncle Sam gets his."

"So you're not flying me off to a remote island paradise? You're the worst dirty old man I've ever seen."

Hurley just shrugged. "Any sausage make it into today's gravy?" When he realized how suggestive his question sounded, he wanted to apologize, but the server was already in the kitchen.

He could hear her cussing and banging dishes around back there.

Brian Beatty

TURKEY NIGHTS

Other Thursday night regulars, the league bowlers, rented their shoes from up behind the bar. Hurley owned his shoes. His secondhand bowling ball — a black sixteen pounder with neon green swirls he kept polished to a bottomless meditative shimmer — felt drilled as if to fit his fat fingers alone, as if machined by fate.

He wondered, sometimes, if its core was made of some sort of weird 1960s hippie magic.

Hurley carried his shoes and mystical bowling ball in a faded burlap seed bag cinched shut with a leather bootlace that also served as a loop handle.

The league occupied only the first four lanes of the bowling alley, so that left the far lane for Hurley and three lanes in between for families with toddlers who still required the gutter bumpers and young teen couples out on school night dates. Homework apparently didn't matter in all homes. Hurley remembered when it did.

Everybody always wound up watching Hurley's lane. He noticed their staring.

Nothing about his form resembled those tiny golden bowlers poised with arms outstretched atop trophies, but he got the job done. He made up for his lumbering approach and spinless release with deadly aim and brute muscle enough the ball zoomed down the lane as if fired out of a cannon.

Though he never used the lighted scoreboard, Hurley played the same game every Thursday.

He simply kept bowling until he got a turkey, three strikes in a row. Then he was finished. Once he'd leveled three full sets of pins back-to-back-to-back, he headed up to the bar for a beer, that week's workout regimen complete.

His celebratory pints always tasted a bit like the disinfectant used in those sad rental shoes.

Hurley was convinced that must be the taste of victory. It wasn't something he'd ever get used to.

About the author

Brian Beatty is the author of five poetry collections: *Magpies and Crows; Borrowed Trouble; Dust and Stars: Miniatures; Brazil, Indiana: A Folk Poem;* and *Coyotes I Couldn't See.* Beatty's writing has appeared in *The American Journal of Poetry, Anti-Heroin Chic, Conduit, CutBank, Evergreen Review, Exquisite Corpse, Gigantic, Gulf Coast, Hobart, McSweeney's, The Missouri Review, Monkeybicycle, The Quarterly, Rattle, Seventeen* and *Sycamore Review.* In 2021 he released *Hobo Radio,* a spoken word album with original music by Charlie Parr. Beatty lives in Saint Paul, Minnesota.

.

Danny Sophabmisay

DWB

Althea Gibbs knew there was something off about the white dude. His mind was elsewhere, his moves were erratic, and on the morning she met him, he would end up changing her life. Forever.

She'd been cleaning out the crap in her garage, where along the back wall was a shelf cluttered with knickknacks, most of them worn and faded and coated in a thin layer of dust. Althea gathered up a handful, then tossed them into a Hefty bag to be taken out with the rest of the trash. There were just a few items that held onto the bad, brutal memories of the past year, and she didn't want to see or touch them again, as if their presence would bring back the trauma and twist the knife in her heart. Digging around, she found a blue cookie tin and hesitated before popping its lid. Inside were the remnants of a young man's life: a half-smoked pack of Newports, service ribbons, one Silver Star, and a dozen photographs. Most of the photos had been snapped in the low deserts of Stanland where the young man commanded his unit.

Snap! He fist bumps a brother-in-arms.

Snap! He stands in front of a Humvee, holding his M4.

Snap! He greets a crowd of bouncing children and smiling villagers.

There was only one photo of him at home in Gary, Indiana, sitting next to his mother with an arm draped around her shoulders. It was also one of the last photos of him ever taken before he took a bullet in the chest.

Captain Devonte Gibbs, Third Regiment, First Division, M.I., was just twenty-seven years old.

Althea decided to put the tin back and toss out her son's exercise bench instead. A diseased rat came scuttling from under it and hissed at her through a set of fang-like teeth. She jumped back and yelped, then turned to her cat, Nubbins, sitting in an empty box and flicking his tail.

"You got nine lives," she said to him. "Would it kill you to chase a couple of rats?"

He looked at her like he couldn't care less.

Outside, the weather was warm and bright, and Althea took a moment to appreciate the scene. She was even tempted to take a deep breath of the air, but knew better. Gary was a cesspool where the U.S. Steel plant produced large amounts of sulfur and smelled like the Devil's asshole. Yet, she believed if she ignored the stench and decay of the city, there was a decent quality to the morning. What made it even nicer was her vehicle parked in the driveway: a 2008 Ford Mustang Bullitt. Althea had bought it brand new and maintained the body ever since. Her love of cars had come from her father who grew up in Detroit, and that love was then passed on to her son.

Like the other reminders, it needed to go. Maybe. Althea had debated it, changed her mind as often as she changed shirts, then put a FOR SALE sign on the windshield. The Mustang was looking cherry that day, and she wasn't the only one to notice its pop.

Enter: the white dude. He looked like a dirty scarecrow — tall, gaunt, and dressed in a sweat-stained work shirt. Every few seconds he glanced over the tattered backpack strapped to his shoulders as he walked up to the car. He didn't seem to notice Althea in the back of the garage. From where she was standing, it looked like he was thinking about stealing it instead of inspecting it. She tried not to think the worst about people, but a cracker on the block got her nerves up.

"Can I help you?" she asked.

The stranger was startled. He straightened himself up and flashed a smile.

"Afternoon, ma'am. Is your husband home?"

"Nope. I don't got a husband. If you're interested in buyin', the old pony's mine."

"Sorry for assumin'," he said. "It's not every day you see a woman with such a, uh, muscular vehicle."

He began to close the distance between them, and Althea met him halfway to get a better look at his mug. He was at a point in life where he could be anywhere from his late-twenties to late-thirties. It all depended on how hard he lived, and the few white dudes left in Gary lived for boozing, brawling, and balling cheap women. Those types of activities aged a man like milk and etched his face with deep lines like the ones he had. Still, he was handsome in a hardened sort of way, sporting a pencil-style mustache and chewing a toothpick. There was also an energy about him, as if he was the one selling the car to her.

"The color sure is pretty," he said.

"Yeah, she was built and painted like the one in Bullitt. Ever see that movie? It's kinda simple but has a lot of style. Same with the car. I named her Queenie."

"Why not McQueen?"

"Don't you know all cars are named after women? Comes from the old sailing days."

"Well, I bet Queenie's somethin' special."

The white dude smiled, and his eyes were alive. Althea studied them for a moment.

"You're not from around here, are you?" she asked.

"No, ma'am, I was just trampin' along. Got a friend who lives a few blocks over, and we share a car to drive for Uber. He was supposed to drop it off at my place, but I guess he had a hot date or somethin'. Anyway, while headin' to his house, I saw your vehicle and figured I'd come in for a closer look, maybe make an offer if you haven't sold her already."

"Haven't yet. Where'd you work before?"

He shrugged. "Here and there. Had a job doin' construction around Crown Point, and I spent some time in Michigan City." Reaching into his pocket, he pulled out a thick wad of cash. "Now if you're worried I'm wastin' your time and don't possess the, uh, funds to purchase this fine motorcar, here's some of my foldin' money."

"You ain't gotta prove you got the money," she said. "Especially by doin' that. This is a bad part of town."

"True, but I didn't want to offend you by clutchin' my purse."

He wiped the sweat off his brow and aired out his shirt. There was definitely something odd about the dude, and it wasn't just the way he talked or twitched. He could be anyone, from a sex maniac to a serial killer, but Althea refused to think that way about him. She wanted him to know she believed in the goodness of people (well, most people) and introduced herself. He shook her hand with a firm, enthusiastic grip.

"I'm Dylan Van Meter," he said. "As much as I enjoy chattin' here, Miss Gibbs, I wouldn't mind gettin' down to business and payin' you cash-money – no paperwork, no bill of sale if it makes it easier for ya – to take Queenie off your hands. I just need to peek under her skirt and give her a ride, if you don't mind."

"As long as you don't mind me goin' with you," she said.

"Of course not." A sly grin played across his face. "I wouldn't trust me to take her 'round the corner without burnin' rubber."

Althea laughed, and for the first time in a long time, she felt a little better about the day ahead.

"Lemme get the keys," she said.

#

Ten minutes later they were on I-94, passing by rows of burnt-out houses and abandoned lots. Dylan sat behind the wheel and gunned the engine. Horsepower: 315. Torque: 325. Althea knew the specs better than any gearhead and listed them off as the car responded to a firm touch of the wheel and hugged the pavement like an old friend. Shifting into fifth, Dylan took it up to 100, and if Althea minded, she didn't say anything. She simply looked out at the highway and felt the thrum of the V8 in her chest.

Dylan laughed. "Hot damn," he said. "She runs like a champ. You sure you don't have anything hidin' under the hood – no supercharger, nitrous, none of that?"

"Not unless they put it in at the factory." Althea held onto the oh-shit-bar as they took the nearest exit ramp and drove downtown where the squat red buildings looked like crumbling souls. Shifting in her seat, she tapped her thighs. "You might want to slow down here. They got speed radars."

"Eh, we'll be all right. A car like this is meant to be driven. And I mean really driven. Don't tell me you only bought her on account of her looks."

"Course not," she said. "You know where Brownsburg is? It's a little town west of Indy and they got a dragstrip for all the race teams there. It's open on Wednesdays – Wild Wednesdays they call it – and I used to go down and pull 12s."

Dylan whistled. "Not bad," he said. "How fast have you taken her on the highway?"

"Seventy. Seventy-five maybe. No more than that, though."

He glanced at her out the corner of his eye. "Say you haven't."

"I haven't."

"You're pullin' my leg."

"I'm not pullin' anything. I've never gone over the speed limit."

"Why not?" A puzzled look came across his face and he started to laugh. "This is a Ford fuckin' Mustang, if you'll excuse the language. How could you not drive it fast?"

"'Cause the police would think I stole it."

Althea bit her words off and the two of them sat in sudden, unexpected silence. The air in the car felt thick. Heavy. Dylan tried to look elsewhere. He had no idea what to do to break the tension, so he said, "Jesus. I'm sorry."

"It happens."

"It shouldn't."

"The world is full of things that shouldn't happen, but do," Althea said. "A white man gets pulled over in a car like this and he's complimented. 'Gee, this sure is a sweet ride, mister. I only stopped you so I could get a better look.' A black man gets pulled over and he's interrogated. 'Where'd you get this car, boy? Show me your license and registration!' It's like he can't own anything but a bucket of bolts or can't drive unless he's off to do crime. I ain't gettin' arrested for DWB."

Dylan asked her what that meant, and Althea told him: "Driving While Black."

"Is that why you're sellin' the car?" he asked.

"Sort of."

"What happened?"

She looked away from him and out the passenger window. "You and me don't need to talk about what was."

There was an edge to her voice she didn't like, and Althea wondered if she should keep quiet about things. It wasn't polite to unload her troubles onto a stranger, but to not talk about them was also bullshit. Why would she care if Dylan learned about the ghost in the machine?

It had happened last summer when Devonte Gibbs came home from nine years of fighting in Stanland. He had plans to get an apartment close to his new job, but in the meantime, he'd been living at home with Althea. One evening, the open road had called to him, and he borrowed Queenie for a cruise. There was no better feeling than cruising – driving at the magic hour with fresh air blowing through the windows and music coming from the radio. He'd been heading towards West 4th Avenue, and according to official reports, swerved a mere six inches into the adjacent lane. Devonte didn't drink, didn't do drugs, and it was likely he'd gotten distracted by a text message (which was later confirmed in court via cellphone records). The swerve was enough for Officer Steven Sharp, though. He'd been tailing Devonte for the past few miles, and once he saw him swerve, he hit the siren. Whoop! Whoop! It was the sound of every black man's worst nightmare, and after hearing it, Devonte used his turn signal to pull over. He had no warrants and the only thing that could possibly be classified as a weapon was a Leatherman that Althea had gotten him as a welcome home present. Still, there must have been something that set the white policeman off, because the moment Devonte had asked him what the problem was, Officer Sharp ordered him out of the vehicle.

He searched him. Hard.

Later in court, the dashcam footage would show the officer was clearly on a power trip. Reddened skin. Tightened muscles. Cords bulging from his neck. In contrast, Devonte was the picture of calm. He'd been in the military since he was eighteen and was programmed to be obedient with a simple "yes, sir" or "no, sir." Perhaps it was because of that etiquette the switch went off in Officer Sharp's head. He had felt patronized, disrespected. His blue uniform wasn't the superhero's cape he'd been told it was. His badge didn't earn him worship. His gun didn't add length to his dick.

After searching Devonte and yelling at him like a coked-up drill instructor, Officer Sharp threw him to the ground. The two began to struggle and Sharp pulled his pistol, firing a single shot into Devonte's chest.

Everyone knew that unless he could be heard on camera calling Devonte Gibbs a nigger, there was no way to prove what was in Officer Steven Sharp's heart. The courts had ruled the shooting "accidental." Sharp was just doing his job, they argued; he was following protocol; he didn't pull a person of color over because of the type of vehicle they were driving.

Yeah. Sure.

Althea had put her hopes and dreams into the Mustang, but now, Devonte was in it too. His death haunted her, and she blamed herself for what had happened. Maybe it was easier to just get rid of the damn thing without Dylan knowing its history. After all, an unarmed black man getting shot and killed by the police was common in America. Coiled in her seat, she decided to smolder and not say anything.

Dylan looked over and noticed how tense she was. Like most guys, he was clueless when it came to emotions but could see she was hurting on the inside. He flicked the turn signal.

"What are you doin'?" Althea asked.

"Pullin' over," he said.

"Why?"

"'Cause you're gonna drive this car like you're supposed to for once."

Steering into a parking lot littered with used condoms and shattered glass, Dylan pulled the emergency brake and idled. He turned to Althea and said, "It'd be a sin for you to sell this car and not feel its speed outside a dragstrip."

Althea agreed but kept silent. She thought about Devonte and about how she wasn't allowed to enjoy certain things because of her complexion. If Dylan was serious about purchasing the Mustang from her, she figured, it would be the last chance to drive Queenie full-out.

"I don't know," she said. "I'd be breakin' the law."

Dylan laughed. "Who doesn't break it? This is outlaw country. George Nelson. John Dillinger. All those old-timey bank robbers sped down these roads in stolen jalopies. It's pretty much tradition."

After a little reluctance, they switched spots in the Mustang and Althea adjusted the driver's seat. She half-expected to see the strobe of red and blue lights the moment she grabbed the steering wheel. That's how it always was: bad shit happened to people like her. She drove out of the parking lot and took a couple of side streets that cut crosswise through the city. Every turn allowed her to test the handling, and once she was comfortable, she jammed her foot on the gas.

Althea was taking things fast for once, but not too fast since safety was a concern. Ten above the speed limit was good enough for her. She smiled, and drove along as if in a dream. The more she accelerated, the more the small knot in her stomach unwound. She was tied to nothing now. No cops. No fear. No death. She was free.

Following a few suggestions from her passenger, she drove past a row of businesses where Dylan spotted a convenience store.

"You mind if we stop here?" he asked. "I want to get a Coke and a couple of scratch-offs."

Althea pulled up front while Dylan unbuckled, dug into his backpack, and asked her if she wanted anything. "Naw, I'm good," she said.

He nodded and his eyes crinkled at the corners. "I'll be no more than a minute."

Staying in the car, Althea hummed and drummed the steering wheel to a beat on the radio. She looked in the rearview mirror, grinning at her reflection. Was this how other people felt all the time? After all these years, how could she find happiness in such a simple thing? Then she realized that was the whole point. She never would have known it without Dylan. Sure, the dude might have been a stranger, a little odd and a little off, but he seemed sincere.

He was a good guy.

#

Dylan Van Meter wasn't a good guy.

If Althea hadn't spotted him in the driveway, he would've stolen her car and hit the convenience store already.

He didn't have time to fuck around. He'd been running on fumes by the time he showed up in Gary, hot and sweaty with the last of the Benzedrine draining from his system. He needed more so he could finish the job and head to Mexico. Adrenaline itself wasn't going to cut it— not when he'd been on the road, trying not to get shot, stabbed, and strung up by drug dealers.

But c'est la vie; the life of an outlaw.

Dylan had always wanted to be a career criminal, and guys like Willie Sutton and Pretty Boy Floyd were his idols. They were gentlemen bank robbers who commanded both fear and respect, and that kind of esteem inspired him to follow suit. Modern banks are a lot different, too much risk and too little reward, so Dylan focused his energies on other heists instead: jewelry stores, concerts, floating casinos. It didn't matter as long as he could score. He just should've been more selective when it came to his partners: Blookie Henderson couldn't pour piss out of a boot with the instructions on the heel. He had a serious junk habit that made him look like a zombie, and it had been his nuts-o idea to raid a heroin den dressed as the DEA.

The raid went off without a hitch, but a bit of research would've told them the stash belonged to Verdell Greene, a mid-level crime boss with a love of violence. Verdell had tracked Blookie down a week after the rip-off, cutting open his stomach and strangling him to death with his own intestines.

Dylan wanted revenge. His plan: squeeze Verdell by taking all the dirty money kept at his drop spots. He had plotted a course and hit two of the three spots in a single night – one in Cleveland, one in Detroit. This convenience store was last on Dylan's list, and he had needed a new set of wheels to get him to El Rey after. When he saw the Mustang, he was set to take it, but the kindness of Althea got to him. She trusted him. Her belief in people was endearing, and Dylan felt a little bad about stringing her along.

Oh well. The job would be quick, and they'd soon be on their separate ways.

His pulse quickened and his palms began to sweat as he entered the convenience store. Behind the counter was a heavy-set clerk wearing a moth-eaten hoodie. The clerk was smiling as he tapped his mobile phone, engrossed in a game and checking out girls on social media. He didn't bother looking at Dylan as the bell above the door chimed and the outlaw prowled the narrow aisles. Eyes still on his phone, the clerk asked if Dylan had cash on him.

"Card reader don't work," he said.

Dylan assured him he had cash as he approached the counter with a small bag of chips and a bottle of pop.

"Everybody claim they got dough but no dollars," the clerk said. "They come in tryna buy Henny and shit. Forget food and baby clothes. Priorities, am I right?"

"Yeah, and yours will be to get your hands up!" Dylan whipped out a .45 automatic and pointed it at the clerk. "Get 'em up! Don't do anything stupid!"

The clerk looked down the barrel of the gun and tried not to shit his pants. He didn't cry. He didn't whimper. He was full of fear, however, and in a low, quiet voice he managed to speak. "Whoa, easy, man. No need to get wild up in here." He held his hands up in surrender, then reached over to open the till. A crumpled wad of bills and blackened coins were set on the counter.

Dylan snapped. "The fuck is this?! I don't want your spare change, man. I want Verdell's money! Don't fuck with me!"

The clerk started to move his hand off the counter in a slow, subtle manner. He was either reaching for his phone to take a pic for the 'Gram (#robbed) or for a weapon. Like a rattlesnake, Dylan struck him in the face with the butt of his gun. A loud crack sounded, and chunky blood spurted out of the clerk's nose like a busted water main. The clerk cupped his hands to collect the blood, snot, and flecks of teeth. "Fuck! Okay," he said. "I'll get it for you! Just no more Bronson stuff, aight? I got kids and shit."

Pinching his nose, he moved around the counter to a walk-in cooler in the back. Frigid air seeped out in a wisp as he opened it and moved a couple racks of Steel Reserve. Behind one of them was a safe. Dylan trained his gun on the clerk in case he got any bright ideas, but the clerk just pulled the safe open. He came out with a leather satchel bulging at the seams, handing it to Dylan.

"You think you're smart, huh?" the clerk asked. "You think we don't know who you are?"

Dylan hit him in the gut, doubled him over. "I'm Dylan Van Meter, and I'm bigger than any criminal who ever lived!"

A booming shotgun blast put an end to their exchange, and two young thugs came out of nowhere. They'd been ordered to keep an eye out for the crazy white guy after Verdell's second spot got hit. After waiting in the back of the store, listening to what was being said, they jumped out clutching their 12-gauges.

Aim wasn't much of a concern for them. They pulled their triggers and sprayed buckshot.

Dylan fired back and ducked out of the convenience store as glass, snack packs, and toiletries exploded all around him.

#

Althea sat and noticed the little details she'd taken for granted: black leather, metallic trim, aluminum shifter. She wanted to capture the feeling of the car before she said goodbye to it forever. Her fingers traced the instrument panel as she sang along to a tune from Soul 106.3, but the sudden crack of a gunshot took her out of the groove. She turned the volume down and listened.

Four more shots went off and Dylan came rushing out of the convenience store, perspiring like a hard-run horse.

Althea looked at him, startled.

"Drive! Drive! Drive!" he said.

He launched himself over the hood, jumped inside, and Althea hit the gas before he could even pull the door shut. The Mustang peeled rubber and sprayed gravel as it lurched forward into traffic. Glancing over, Althea saw Dylan holding onto a leather satchel like a kid with their favorite stuffed animal. She knew what he'd been up to and was almost tempted to stop driving but threw her eye to the rearview mirror. Two gun-toting hoods came bounding out of the store. One of them fired off a thundering shot, and the back windshield shattered with Althea turning the wheel and riding a curb.

"Lord I knew it!" she said. "Deep down, I knew you was shady, but I was bein' nice and let you test drive Queenie. What'd you do, Dylan? I mean, what were you even thinkin' when you went in there?!"

He wiped the sweat off his brow and rooted through the satchel. "It's a long story and I ain't gotta explain it. Right now, I need you to be cool, Miss Gibbs."

"I am cool."

She continued to speed but was gripping the steering wheel for a different reason: she didn't like being lied to. Althea's kindness had been exploited, and Dylan didn't seem too concerned that she was now his getaway driver. He didn't seem too concerned about the men gunning after them either. He looked inside the satchel and smiled at the banded stacks of hundreds.

For him, it wasn't about cash-value. Verdell Greene was paying for what he did to Blookie.

A distant police siren cut through the deep growl of the engine, and Althea stiffened. "That for us?"

"Could be. Not too many people call the cops 'round here, even if someone did get shot."

"You shot somebody?!"

Dylan ignored the question and pointed ahead. "Turn here. We can lose 'em real quick."

A sharp curve showed up and Althea drifted into it, shooting straight down the road and blowing through a red light.

"We're not gonna get away with it," she said.

"Not with that attitude." Dylan checked the side mirrors and saw they were in the clear. He saw Althea shake her head slowly. "Miss Gibbs, look at me," he said. She turned and saw the sincerity in his eyes. "I'm sorry," he continued. "I really am. I didn't mean to bring you into this mess, and I'm gonna make sure you get out of it, all right?"

She raised an eyebrow and thought if Dylan was capable of what he did in the convenience store, who knew what else he was capable of. It seemed like ages ago they were driving around as newfound friends, and, in a way, she still felt they were. "Okay, but what about the cops?" she asked. "What if they find out I'm the driver and question me?"

"They're not gonna find out."

"But if they do, how can you be sure I'll be quiet about it?"

"I can't be, but I trust you anyway."

Dylan suggested a narrow alleyway for them to duck into, and Althea parked behind a graffitied dumpster. They both fell silent, staring ahead. Letting out a breath, Althea bent forward, then stretched the tension out of her body. Certain thoughts were forming in her mind, and she tried not to beat herself up over them. She needed to make peace and accept that she had become involved in a crime by happenstance, one that had carried her away for a minute and was sort of exciting.

"So what happens now?" she asked.

"You can report the car stolen if you want. I'm still gonna drive her for as long as I can."

They climbed out of the Mustang with Dylan getting behind the wheel and Althea remaining outside. The chase had ended, but for some reason, they both lingered in the trash-strewn alley.

"You okay?" Dylan asked.

"I don't know," Althea said. "I feel kinda guilty."

"You shouldn't. You did what you had to do, and you did a damn fine job." Reaching behind the seat, he pulled out his backpack. "Here," he said. He handed it to Althea and watched her wonder over what was inside. "I don't know what Kelley Blue Book thinks she's worth...but that's what I think."

Her jaw dropped when she saw all the loot he'd stolen from the first two drop spots. Every time Althea dipped into the backpack, she came out with another stack of hundred-dollar bills. A smile pushed upward as she realized the total had to be in the high six-figures. No amount was enough to take back what happened, or what had happened, but it was enough to pay off any lingering debts. She zipped up the backpack and held it by its straps. "This is too much," she said.

"Miss Gibbs, I know that Queenie's got some bad memories in her, but try to think of this as one of the better ones," he said. "You can get yourself a new set of wheels with that. Maybe a Cadillac."

"Or maybe somethin' faster," she said. And she would. The getaway was enough of an experience to embolden her on the open road. Bold enough, at least, to go a few miles over the speed limit like everyone else. Althea let out a small laugh. "You know, I always thought the Trans Am from Smokey and the Bandit was pretty cool."

"Sure is."

Dylan rested his left arm on the windowsill and looked at her with a warm smile. Althea grinned mischievously as he shifted the Mustang into first and watched him ride off into the morning sun, feeling exhausted and not quite wrapping her thoughts around the fact she was never going to see him or Queenie again.

About the author

Danny Sophabmisay is just happy to be here. His stories have appeared in *Switchblade* and *Hoosier Noir*.

Matthew X. Gomez
RUST BELT REVENANT

Tim Mulligan never saw the car coming. It came from a blind spot, hitting the passenger side hard. Next, he knew he was getting punched in the face by the airbag, and hearing Sara, his wife of five years crying out. They were on their way back from their anniversary dinner at a quiet, out of the way restaurant. He had pulled on to the back road leading to their house when the other car hit them, sending them sliding off into the ditch at the side of the road.

"Sara?" he asked. Something wet dripped down into his eyes. He raised his hand and wiped away the blood. He heard his wife groan. "Sara, baby, are you okay?"

"Tim? I...I can't move my arm. Or my legs." He looked over. The side of the car was crumpled, the dashboard pushed forward, trapping her.

"Okay, hold on." He managed to pull his cell phone from his pocket, thankfully still intact. He swiped up and tried to dial 911, but no luck. No signal out this way. That was one of the things they liked living out in the country.

He unlocked his door and nearly fell out when he opened it, saved only by his seat belt. He unhooked it, and got unsteadily to his feet. He saw the headlights from the other car on the road. He rubbed his eyes. Yeah, two figures were silhouetted against the night sky.

"Hey, can one of you call for help? My wife is trapped down here."

"You both all right?" one of them asked. Tim thought the voice familiar, but he couldn't quite place it.

"We need medical attention," Tim shouted back.

One of the figures came down the embankment.

"Dwight?" Tim asked. "What are you doing out here? You guys drunk? You ran us off the road!"

Dwight stumbled and cursed and slid on his ass the rest of the way down. He shone a flashlight at Tim for a moment before playing it over the car.

"Shit, that Sara?" Dwight asked. "Hey Kev, Sara's down here too."

"Kevin? Seriously Dwight, what are you two doing out here? Anyway, you have to help me with Sara. She's trapped."

Dwight shook his head. "Real shame. I always liked Sara."

"Wait, what?"

Tim didn't see Dwight pull the gun. He didn't hear the gunshot. He found himself on the ground, in pain, bleeding. He saw Dwight walking over to the car.

"No, please. Dwight. She had nothing to do with it."

Dwight paused. Looked over at Tim. Tim couldn't see his face in the dark, couldn't tell if he looked sorry or angry or mean or even sad. He saw his shadowy bulk walk to the car. He heard a voice, muffled. Sara's.

He heard the gunshot.

Footsteps shuffled through the leaves back to him. A light shone in his face, bright enough to force him to squeeze his eyes shut.

"Still alive, Tim?" Dwight asked.

"Why?"

Dwight chuckled. "You got the nerve to ask me that? Mr. Caruso figured out what you were doing, Tim. Thought you were being smart, skimming off a bit for yourself, didn't you? Didn't think you'd get caught, huh? Not so smart now, are you?"

Tim coughed and spat blood. "This is what this is all about?" He tried to lift his arm, but it was not accepting the signal from his brain. He figured he did not have too much longer. "Because I stole from that fat fuck?"

Dwight knelt and angled the flashlight out of Tim's face. "Yeah, maybe. You think he tells people like Kevin and me the reasons? Fuck no. But, well, if you stole from him, and he figured it out, I'd say that was as good a reason as any."

"But Sara. Why her?"

"Collateral damage man. Should have thought about that before doing whatever it was you did."

Dwight stood up and walked away. Tim could hear him stumbling through the underbrush, heard him curse, saw the light bob and weave as he made his way back to the road. He closed his eyes, felt the hot tears on his face. He did not weep for himself, but for his wife. She never asked about work, or where the extra money came from. But she did not deserve this. How long would it take for anyone to find them? Would there ever be any justice?

"No."

Tim blinked. "What? Who's there?"

A figure emerged from the trees. Tall, with a long coat or cloak trailing behind them. The figure moved effortlessly in the dark and foliage. Tim realized that she did not make a noise as she walked.

"Great. Hallucinating in my final moments."

The figure stopped and sat down across from Tim. He guessed her a woman, all dressed in dark blues with silver accents. A veil the color of old bone concealed her face, and he had this irrational fear that if he saw what she really looked like it would snap what little remained of his frail sanity.

She reached out a pale, nearly skeletal hand, and slapped him hard in the face.

"Ow!"

"Can a hallucination do that?" the woman asked. Her voice sounded like a snake sliding across dry leaves.

"Suppose not. Were you standing there the entire time?" he asked. "You could have called 911."

"No signal, remember? Anyway, I am not what you would call the helpful sort. At least, not for the living."

"So, what then? Hear to keep me company until I bleed out?"

"Technically you're already dead," the woman replied. "I'm here to offer you a deal."

Tim blinked, but had to wonder if the woman was right. He did not hurt anymore. He still could not move, but that was a small thing now.

"What kind of deal?"

"A balancing of accounts. Those men took something from you, something of far more value than what you took from them. I can help you."

Tim searched his feelings, but they all felt distant and removed, like a sheet of ice had formed between his rational and emotional self.

"What do you want from me?"

The woman cocked her head to the side. "I need you to say, 'Yes.'"

"Simple as that then?" he asked.

"Well, a little more complicated than that, but do you see many options for yourself?"

"No. Fine. Yes. I accept."

He could not tell if the woman smiled, but he felt like she did. She darted her hand forward and buried it in his stomach. He felt searing cold, cold enough to burn, and he opened his mouth wide in a soundless scream. The cold spread, from his torso to his limbs to his head, and then he did let out a scream — a wordless, primal tortured cry that echoed through the woods. Then the pain was gone, quick as a snuffed candle, but the feeling of cold remained. He lay there for a moment, afraid to try to move, to do anything at all.

"Go on, get up," the woman said.

Tim struggled to his feet, amazed that the pain had vanished. He stared down at his body, the bullet wound gone, replaced by a bit of blackened flesh that looked like frostbite. His shirt still looked a murder scene, though he guessed that was apt. He walked to the car, refused to look inside. The trunk had popped open during the crash, but one of the suitcases was still in there. Ignoring the woman, he pulled out a change of clothes, used what he had been wearing to wipe himself down as best he could. He stuffed a few belongings into a smaller shoulder bag.

"No chance of you magicking me a cab?" he turned and asked, but the woman was gone.

"Well, shit."

#

Morning found Tim stepping down from the back of a pickup truck at a gas station. The driver had been kind enough to drive him into Montpelier in exchange for fifty bucks. Sure, it was practically highway robbery, but it was not as if Tim really needed the cash. He did not feel hungry or tired or anything except an abiding sense of anger.

"Uh, can I help you?" the pimple faced teen behind the glass partition asked.

"I need to buy a gallon of gas. Wait. No. Two."

"Okay. Jugs are behind you. You pay here and then fill it up outside. Car break down?"

"Something like that," Tim replied. He bought the gas and a ball cap and a pair of cheap sunglasses before heading back outside to get his bearings. Montpelier was not all that big, and he figured nobody would be looking for him, especially not his erstwhile employer. He donned the cap and sunglasses jus the same. He felt a pull, like a leash around his neck, in three separate directions. He hefted the gas cans and followed the strongest pull.

He found himself standing across the street from a single-family home. Overgrown weeds in the front yard. Fence in need of a new coat of paint. Two cars in the driveway, one of them up on blocks. The closest neighbors were screened by a row of hedges grown wild. He crossed the street and circled around to the back. A lawn gone to seed. A rusted-out grill. A woodpile with who knew what living in it.

Definitely Kevin's place.

Tim set down the gasoline and picked up one of the sturdier pieces of wood. He smacked it on the ground a couple of times to make sure it would not crumble upon impact. Satisfied, he went to one of the back windows. He broke the window, then paused, listening for movement from within. Hearing nothing, he cleared the rest of the glass way and unlatched it. Tim was not a big man, but he still struggled a bit to get through. For a moment he wondered what it would look like if Kevin caught him like that, half in and half out of the window. What would he do, seeing a dead man trapped like that?

It did not come to that, however, and he managed to slip inside undiscovered. He moved through the house, quiet as a church mouse. He entered the garage and did not find Kevin, but he did pick up a claw hammer that felt right in his hand. Moving further into the house he found Kevin, passed out on the couch. Some schlock b-movie horror was playing on the television, empty cans of beer scattered across the room and some cold pizza sat on a coffee table, still in the box. A gun sat on the couch next to him. Tim picked it up and checked it. Loaded.

"Wake up, Kevin," Tim said, kicking him hard in the leg.

Kevin woke up, spluttering, reaching for the gun that was not there.

"Tim?" he asked.

"Got it in one, big guy."

"But Dwight said he shot you. Said you were dying. How come you're here?"

"Think about it Kevin. Think long and hard. You watch horror, right? What do you think happens next?"

"No. No. Look. It was not my idea, all right? I was just the driver. Just following orders. You can't hold that against me, can you?"

Tim brought the hammer around is a downward arc. Kevin had enough time to get his arm up in the way. It broke with a wet crack.

"Ahh, my arm, you sick fuck!" He tumbled from the couch to the floor, cursed again when he landed on his arm. He started to crawl away. "You wait, Tim, just wait. Mr. Caruso will hear about this. Then you will be in trouble.

Tim threw the gun onto the couch and jumped on top of Kevin. He grabbed a fistful of hair and yanked his head back, brought the hammer up. He took a moment to flip it around, then drove the claw part down into Kevin's head. He stood up, leaving the hammer buried, its purpose served. Kevin's body twitched, the last electronic signals from the brain to the body that did not know it was dead already.

"What's he going to do Kevin? Kill me again?"

He took the pistol from the couch, stuck it in the waistband of his pants. It was not something he would have ever done back when he was still alive, but he could not see much risk of it now.

He exited the house, pausing only to collect the car keys hanging from a hook by the back door. He grabbed the gasoline cans and placed them in the backseat. He closed his eyes, wanting to feel something at Kevin's death. Remorse, maybe. Self-loathing? Accomplishment?

Nothing.

He drove slow through the town. Taking it in. Not yet a ghost town but moving in that direction. Too many people leaving, not enough staying. And for what? No real prospects. Nothing to make a career out of. He liked it because of the quiet. People minding their own business, for the most part. And where had that got him? College degree and the only job he could get was working for the local loan shark and heroin supplier. More houses looked like Kevin's then not. He could not even blame people like Caruso. Healthy systems tended to reject parasites. Weakened ones lacked the defense to keep them out. And his own weakness had led him to working for the man, and his greed had led to him stealing from an employer who was more likely to leave you dead in a ditch than give you a pink slip.

He arrived out front of Dwight's home. His lawn was better kept, how home in better repair. Two cars out front, but both in good shape. Tim parked down the block and watched a while. He saw Kevin's wife, Sheila, if he remembered right, walk out of the house with two kids and a mess of sports equipment. They piled into one of the cars, a wagon. Goodbyes were shouted, and then they were gone, off to some game or other. For a brief, mad moment, Tim thought about following them, running them off the road. He thought about driving them into a ditch then calling Dwight, telling him where could find his family.

No.

He shook his head.

That was not him.

Instead, he walked up the front walk, making sure his gun was hidden by his shirt. He thought he saw the curtains at one of the neighbors' twitch. Not that it mattered. He knocked on the door.

"One moment!" he heard Dwight call out. No fancy device for him to see who was waiting on his front door. Not even the sense of self-preservation to look through the peephole first. When you were the right hand of the meanest son-of-a-bitch in town, who would come after you?

The door opened. Tim drew the gun.

"Tim?" Dwight blinked, mouth hanging open. He did not register the gun.

Tim shot him in the leg. The neighbor was probably fumbling for the phone right now, hustling to call the police. That did not give Tim much time, but he did not need much.

Dwight fell backwards with a cry. "Tim... wait, oh, fuck, wait... it's not... I didn't... how..."

Tim forced a smile on his face. He raised the gun. He pulled the trigger.

As he drove away in Kevin's car, he heard the sirens approaching in the distance, but he knew the roads well enough to not pass them. One last string pulled at his next. Kevin had driven the car and Dwight had fired the gun, but they were instruments of another. The man who ordered the hit was still out there, one last account to be balanced.

As he drove, the veiled woman appeared in the passenger seat next to him. "I thought you would drag the killings out more."

"Why?"

"Because of what they did to you. What they did to your wife. Would that not make you feel better?"

Tim shook his head. "I thought it would. But I don't feel much of anything. Side effect of dying and coming back?"

"Who said anything about you coming back?" the woman asked.

"So, I'm dead then?"

"Not quite. More like caught in between two states."

"Huh. So does that..." He trailed off as she was gone again.

It was lunch time when he arrived at Caruso's. The front was a tax preparation business, shuttered except by appointment only most of the year. Not a bad set up, Tim had to admit. He could see his desk through the window. They had not boxed up his belongings yet. Probably waiting for the police to declare him officially missing, and maybe waiting a bit longer than that before an anonymous call informed them of where to find the wreck. Long enough that decomposition would handle some of the messy work, make it hard to reconstruct what had happened.

He parked the car in front of the office. Leaving the gas cans in the car for the moment, he stepped out, keys dangling in his hand. Why bother to change the locks? The door chime announced his arrival.

"Kevin? Dwight? That you?" he heard a voice call from the back. "Be... uhh... right with you."

"Guess again," Tim called out. He held Kevin's gun loose in his hand.

"Tim?" Gina, Caruso's secretary and mistress, stepped out of a backroom, smoothing down her skirt and adjusting her blouse. "What- you look like shit."

Tim nodded. "Yeah. I expect I do. Go on. Get out. You don't want to be here."

Tim stood to one side and pushed open the door to Caruso's office. A double blast from a shotgun ripped through the air, left his ears ringing. He came into the room, hard and fast. Caruso fumbled with the shotgun, spilling shells on the floor as he struggled to reload it. Tim went around the desk, pressed the barrel of the pistol against Caruso's temple and pulled the shotgun from his hands, tossing it on the floor.

"Dwight said he killed you. Guess he was wrong."

Tim shook his head. "Not... entirely."

"What?"

"Handcuffs, top drawer, am I right?"

Caruso frowned at him but opened the drawer. Under a manilla folder were the handcuffs. "How'd you know?"

"Three years ago, we went out partying. You bragged how you liked to cuff a girl, kept a set on hand in case the mood struck you. Your turn to wear them. Hands behind your back."

"Is this about money? Look I can give you money. The safe is right there." Caruso closed the cuff around one wrist, then the other, behind his back.

"It's not about the money." He wondered if Gina was calling the police. Or trying to call Caruso's lieutenants. Either way, he did not have much time. "I'll be right back."

Walking outside of the office, he saw Gina standing against the wall, taking long drags on a cigarette.

"You kill him?" she asked.

Tim raised an eyebrow at her. "No. Well, not yet."

She watched him go to the car, get out the gasoline cans. "That's Kevin's car," she observed. "What happened to the front?"

"There was an accident."

"An accident or an on purpose?"

Tim looked long and hard at her. "You don't want to be here."

She nodded, dropped the cigarette, and ground it out under her heel. "Yeah." She opened her purse, fished around in it for a bit and pulled out a lighter. She strutted over to Tim, pushed it into the pocket of his pants. "I liked you, you know? Not enough to mess up what you and Sara had going on, but... Look. Whatever happened, I'm sorry."

Tim closed his eyes and heard her walk away. He heard a car door open and close, heard the engine start, heard it pull away. When he reopened them, she was gone.

"Nice girl," said the veiled woman. She leaned against the hood of

Kevin's car. Tim could not help but notice she did not cast a shadow. "Are you ready?"

Tim walked back into the office. Caruso was where he had left him, only now his face was beaded with sweat, dress shirt sticking. His dark eyes were wide and darting, and only got wider when he saw what Tim was carrying.

"What, no. No. This isn't right, this isn't the way it's supposed to go."

Tim splashed the gasoline from both cans over the desk and floor and over Caruso, who spluttered and cursed and coughed and begged. Once both cans were empty, he grabbed the wastepaper basket, already half-full. He grabbed the lighter, sparked it to life.

"That's Gina's lighter. What, did you kill her too? You asshole!" Caruso screamed.

Tim flicked the lighter. Stared at the flame for a minute. "She doesn't love you." He set the paper on fire, tossed the basket into the gas-soaked room, and ran.

Twenty miles down the road, driving with the windows down, some classic rock from the '70s blaring on the stereo, and the veiled woman appeared in the passenger seat.

"So that's it the, yeah?" Tim asked.

"What makes you say that?" the woman asked.

"I killed them. The ones that did me wrong. Dwight and Kevin and Caruso. What's left? Don't I get to move on? Don't I get to be with Sara?" He felt something akin to sadness take over him, but it was dim and distant. A candle flickering on a foggy night.

"Whoever said you get to move on?" the veiled woman said. "That was never part of our agreement."

Tim frowned and stared ahead at the vanishing road, wishing he could muster sadness or anger or bitter regret. Something other than the pale emotion he felt now that was simple disappointment. For a moment, he thought about yanking the wheel to the side, ending it all, but the woman placed her ice-cold hand on top of his and steadied the wheel.

"You belong to me now," she said, and Tim knew there would be no easy out for him.

About the author

Matthew X. Gomez can be found on twitter @mxgomez78. Other work of his has appeared in *Pulp Modern, KZINE, Econoclash Review,* and *Grimdark*. He released his first collection of fiction *God in Black Iron and Other Stories* in 2020.

ABOUT HOOSIER NOIR

Hoosier Noir is an imprint exploring Indiana authors and stories, focusing primarily on crime but inclusive of other forms of dark fiction. This is the fifth volume published since Hoosier Noir began in 2020.

You can find more information, including submissions calls, on our Twitter (@hoosiernoir) and find volumes 1-4, and our 4:20 Noir special on Amazon.

We thank all our readers for their support, and hope you enjoyed Hoosier Noir Vol. 5.

84

www.ingramcontent.com/pod-product-compliance
Lightning Source LLC
Chambersburg PA
CBHW071942120726
48001CB00005B/1999